Clint Faraday

book twenty seven
A Wreath for Sam

Sam Martin answers a call at the front door. A woman from a flower delivery service announces, "A wreath for Sam!"

He was the only Sam there – and he wasn't dead.

Contents

About the author

CD Moulton has traveled extensively over much of the world both in the music business, where he was a rock guitarist, songwriter and arranger and in an import/export business. He has been everything from a bar owner to auto salvage (junkyard) manager, longshoreman to high steel worker, orchid grower to landscaper, tropical fish farmer to commercial fisherman. He started writing books in 1983 and has published more than 350 books as of January 1, 2023. His most popular books to date are about research with orchids, though much of his science fiction and fantasy work has proven popular. He wrote the CD Grimes, PI series, and the Det. Nick Storie series, Clint Faraday series, and many other works.

He now resides in Gualaca, Chiriqui, Panamá, where he writes books, plays music with friends, does research with orchids and medicinal plants. He has lately become involved in fighting for the rights of the indigenous people, who are among his closest friends, and in fighting the extreme corruption in the courts and police in Panamá.

He offers the free e-book, *Fading Paradise*, that explains what he has been through because of the corruption.

CD is the discoverer of the Chadam Protocol for curing cancer.

Facebook page Ambrosia peruviana for cancer.

A Wreath for Sam

Delivery

Clint Faraday, retired PI from Florida now living in Bocas del Toro, Panamá, sighed deeply and shook his head. Jaime, a close friend and neighbor, was complaining about Gina, a woman he met last night at The Lemon Grass restaurant had just left him. She had seemed an intelligent woman when she came to talk with him. She was interesting and had been a few places he had been.

Dave, his nutty musician/writer/botanist friend was playing with some of the local musicians and had warned Jaime that she was a flake. He thought she was bipolar or something.

She had seemed very nice. He should learn to listen to friends like Dave, who was blunt to the point of being obnoxious, at times, but was a true friend.

It was a great night, really. It just wasn't a very good morning after. He woke up a lot earlier than she did and went to his regular routine – lots of coffee, a couple hojaldras, some liver and onions this morning, half a muskmellon, lay in his hammock awhile to watch the sunrise, swim for fifteen or twenty minutes, get dressed for the day.

She woke up about nine fifteen and started almost screaming at him for not getting her up at seven thirty. He answered that she didn't tell him she wanted to get up at any specific time, so he let her sleep.

She said she'd probably missed her bus to Boca del Drago. Thanks heaps for ruining her whole day before it even got started!

"There's another bus every hour this early, so what's the big deal? All you had to do was say you wanted to get up at seven and I would get you up at seven. I'm awake at four thirty."

"You stinking damned son of a bitch! You get me drunk and take advantage of me, then fuck up my day! Thank you so very damned much!

"In the first place, you came on to me. In the second place, you had one lousy margarita. In the third place, you came out to the cab and here at your own suggestion, not mine. In the forth place you can leave anytime you like, and I would have gotten you up if you'd said something.

"You're weird! Go. Have a nice day, and don't come back. I was warned about you, but didn't listen. That won't happen again!

"Get dressed and get out!"

"So now I don't even get any breakfast? You're a real winner, you are!"

"You want breakfast? It's right there on the stove."

"Well! I don't have time to eat anything now, do I? How about if I go to the police and report you raped me?"

"Have a go at it! You might find I'm not so easy to manipulate with that crap. Ten people saw you come after me and get in the cab on your own."

"And if I tell them I said no, but you screwed me anyway?" she said, with a smirk. "How about then, hotshit?"

"Let's see. You chased me and got in the cab at one o'clock in the morning and came here with me, then said no? That your story?"

"You got it!"

"Give it a shot, but that will fly like a lead kite. They'll laugh you out of town! This isn't the states, where some whore can go to a guy's room at three in the morning and claim rape when she doesn't get paid."

"Are you calling me a whore?!"

"Depends on definitions. You'll be late for the bus if you have to spend all that time at the police station. Better get started."

"I won't go to the police. I just said that."

"Go anyway."

She burst out in tears. "Why do you asshole guys always treat me this way?"

"You really need help. If you forgot to take your lithium or something, take it. If it's not something you're in treatment for, get help. Brother! Do you need it!"

She got a hard mean look as Judi and Clint came to the door behind her. She was just saying, "We'll see how you like *this*, bastard!"

She tore the top of her blouse and screamed, "Help! Help me!"

"Get a grip, bitch!" Judy said, behind her. She staggered and looked scared.

"Oh, God!" she cried. "He tried to rape me!"

"Yeah, right. I was standing right here for the last few minutes and heard the whole thing," Judi snarled. "A friend told me you pulled this kind of crap in Las Tablas. Badger game. He paid you five hundred bucks to go away. We're used to your type of traveling whore here. I suggest you don't try it again in Panamá or you'll end up with free room and board for two years. Got it?"

"Oh, God! I don't have any money and owe the hotel! I was just trying to get enough to pay the bill there."

"You spent the entire five bills in three days? In Panamá?"

She looked cagy. "I was robbed! This guy in

Santiago came into my room at the hotel and, and just took my purse!"

"You reported that to the police?" Clint asked.

"Well, I was scared, see, and he was pretty dangerous looking. I just got the hell out of there and came here!"

"He got your purse and all your identification and such? That's terrible!" Judi said, with a wink at Clint.

"Yes! I don't have *anything* left now, and I'm desperate!"

"I'll tell you something, you dumb half-assed bitch," Judi replied, conversationally. "Clint here is a multi-millionaire and would have been more than glad to help you if you hadn't pulled this stupid act! You can't say a whole sentence without a lie in it. Jaime would have agreed to pay you for the night if you'd simply asked, or he'd say no.

"You didn't come here with no identification and you don't owe anything to any hotel. They're all cash in advance here. Get the hell out or I'll damned well see you locked away for awhile. If you try this act again, I guarantee you're *gone*!"

She bit her lip and started to say something. Judi snarled, "You leaving, or am I gonna *send* you?"

She threw her head back, started to reply, then marched out.

"Weird!" Clint said. "I've seen a lot of weird ones, but she takes the cake!"

"She's a type. Thinks she's in the states and can pull this crap and get away with it. She knows it doesn't work with the natives, so she tries it on gringos. She'll try to spread some kind of story about you now, Jaime. I'll see it smacks her in the puss.

"I have to go to Panamá City today. Anything you need while I'm there?"

"Not very much happening here. I might go to Rambala for a day or two. Nothing I can think of."

They chatted for a few minutes, then Clint and Judi went to their own homes.

Clint was telling Tyna, his wife, about it when the phone rang. Clint answered.

"Mr. Faraday? This is Samuel Martin. I met you at the Ultima Refugio about a week ago. I live just a little before Pastore?"

"Yes. I remember. You're into home furnishing and appliances, if I remember correctly. Main store is in Changuinola, with branches in Almirante and Chiriqui Grande."

"Yes. I bought that finca from Carlos.

"Mr. Faraday, something strange happened. I don't know if it's just a mistake or ... something else."

"Strange?"

"Yes. I just had a funeral wreath delivered this morning. It was brought to the house. I don't know why."

"No one you knew died in the last few days? Who was the wreath for? Whose funeral?"

"That's what's so strange! The delivery woman came to the door and said, 'A wreath for Sam!' and wanted me to sign for it."

"I see. You hadn't ordered any wreath."

"I looked at the card. It said, *Sam Martin. Viaje con Dios. He wouldn't listen.*

"I'm the only Sam Martin I know! I think it must be some kind of warning or threat, but I don't know from whom, or why! It was sent to this address, so it wasn't a mistaken ... you can see why I'm concerned about it."

"What do you want me to do?"

"I don't know that, either. Could you find out who sent it? Maybe they'll tell you why."

Clint considered. He didn't have anything else to do, so why not?

"I'll come over in a couple of hours. Will you be at your home?"

"I'll be here until two."

"Okay."

Martin had fixed up the house very nicely. It was very high-ceilinged and airy. When Carlos built it, there was no electric service for several kilometers. He had put in solar. Lines were going into the area now, but Martin had opted for the solar, because it left him independent. He had added a large terrazzo terrace in front. There were dozens of varieties of tropical fruits on the place. There was a little stream from the mountains across the Changuinola carretera that passed through to the bay. The house was mostly concrete block and steel with a fiberglass terra cotta design roof. A small cottage was toward the stream and lower. It was made of nispero and cedar. Very attractive.

Martin was Panamanian, a very handsome man in his early fifties. He introduced Clint to a very pretty Indigena, about thirty five, as his wife, Emilia. He had a son, Jon, fourteen years old, and daughter, Marta, twelve. They were in the school in Pastore.

He showed Clint a large funeral wreath made with yellow calla lilies and red ginger flowers that featured a large black bow in the center. The card read, as Martin said on the phone, *Sam Martin. Viaje con Dios. He wouldn't listen.*

"There has to be a clue in that. Listen to what?" Clint asked.

"I don't know! This seems to be some kind of threat, but about what? By whom?"

"Business rivals? Money laundering? You have a successful business, so the cartels will try to get you to launder money."

"It is very well known that I have no patience with those kinds. They leave me alone. There is a system in place that tells them who would be interested. They think they set it up, but ... we allow them to think that. I have a fine family, and would not want them ever exposed to the dangers inherent in those dishonest dealings. I am quite comfortable, as you can see. I do not want or need more than I have. I do not wish to know those people. My life is not complicated, and I would aim to keep it that way."

"Very smart. I have to deal with those people far too often.

"I'll try to trace backward from the wreath. Someone paid for it and had it delivered here."

"Yes. It was ordered through Matilde's Flower Boutique in Panamá City, who had Arende's Hauling and Delivery bring it here. That was on the factura I signed when I received it."

"I can work backward from there. I'll need a clear copy of the factura."

"It is here. You may take it. I know you will have it for me if it proves to be important for any other matter." He handed Clint a standard receipt book page. It didn't say much, other than it was ordered and paid by Matilde's Flower Boutique, shipped via Arende's Hauling and Delivery, and was signed as received by Samuel Martin J.

Clint talked few more minutes, but nothing new occurred to Martin. He drove back to Almirante and to Arende's. He didn't learn much there. All they knew was that they made a prepaid delivery to Martin. The package arrived at Changuinola on the early flight, and was delivered to them, they sent it on, it was received and signed. Next stop!

He though a bit. Judi was going to Panamá City this morning, probably caught the early flight and was there by now. He called her and asked that she check on Matilde's Flower Boutique. The order number was on the receipt he had, so she could trace it if she had the time.

There was nobody like Judi Lum for finding information when he needed it! He wondered how much extra he was going to get this time.

This would have to wait until he had something

more. It would probably be to his advantage to learn what he could about his employer of the moment. All he really knew at this point was that Martin owned some stores or something and had bought the place from Carlos and had finished the construction.

He drove to Changuinola and by the largest almacen Martin owned, a few blocks from the downtown area, in a higher income community. It was modern, and featured some very good quality furniture in the display window.

He parked and went inside. It was set up much the same as Elmec, in David. It was strictly high-end furnishings, as well as the better quality building materials. It was roomy, as opposed to the more general bazaar-type established, with things piled high all over the place and barely room to move between the tables. There were three groups of people looking at things, one a local builder.

Clint knew the builder, Moises Silva, so talked with him for a few minutes. He was building an expensive estate house on the other side of the river. They wanted marble baths and a Jacuzzi, plus fancy ostentatious fixtures all over the place. A large crystal chandelier and hand-carved mahogany dining table and chairs and a kitchen with real marble counters. All rooms triple size or larger.

"He won the lottery a couple of months ago, and will run out of money before this is done, if I'm not fast. It's all pay in advance. He'll spend a couple of million on the place. In two years you can buy it for six or eight hundred grand."

"How much did he win, for Christ's sake?"

"About a million."

"And he's prepaid two already?"

"Uh-huh."

"Have the serial numbers been checked?"

Moises laughed. "Direct transfer from his bank to mine. My part's legit. I don't care where he got his."

That was one of the schemes to launder money. Spend two million to legitimize one. Standard deal.

"You won't be able to buy it for anything less than five million. They'll sell it to themselves."

"Is that the place near the bend in the river?"

"Yeah. What?"

"Big glass front, looking at the river? All the rooms ten times a reasonable size?"

"Yeah."

"They'll use this to launder six or eight mil, then open a casino and fancy whorehouse they can use to launder fifty mil a year."

"You're probably right."

"You know Martin, who owns this place?"

"Yeah. He's no part of anything like that. He's made it known that it would be a horrible mistake to try to involve him in anything crooked. He has a family, and they're happy with things as they are."

"Is he religious, do you know?"

"No. He says he doesn't need any church to tell him what's right or wrong – with which I agree."

"Yo tambien."

"Catch you later! Ciao!"

Clint went out to his car to drive around Changuinola to look over the two other smaller stores Martin owned, then back to Almirante to look at the new store there. Everything seemed legitimate. Everyone liked and respected Martin. He was a regular guy. No one had a gripe with him or knew of anyone else who did.

It was looking like this was a mistake, that the wreath must be for some other Samuel Martin. It could still be dangerous if that funeral wreath was meant as a warning or threat. After the wrong person's dead, it doesn't help anything to say, "Oops! Sorry about that!"

He had to be missing something.

Clint knew enough about the business to start an investigation, but there was no direction for it. There was too much he didn't know.

Who was Samuel Martin J. and exactly how was he involved in whatever it was?

Clint went back to Almirante, got his boat, and went on to Bocas Town. He could expect a call from Judi soon. It might give him an idea about what's happening. He wouldn't get anything from the regular crowd. They wouldn't know about this. It was something that had to do with the mainland.

After spending a couple of hours cutting what little grass he had and trimming the shrubbery, a weekly job, where everything grew so fast year around, he swam off his deck for a few minutes, then showered.

He checked his e-mail to find one was from Judi.

Clint – I have checked with the florist. The wreath was sent by a Rudolfo Gomez Cruz. The bill was paid with a credit card, Visa, in the name of Generoso Flores Lorenz. I checked on Gomez: he is a gofer for Flores, who owns a large construction materials distributor (GFL Top-line Industrial Supplies) among other things. He is in Panamá City out toward the causeway. I also talked with some people who knew Martin when he lived in Penonomé. They said he was the type of solid person who was welcomed in the better neighborhoods. The only problem was that he was married to an Indigena while the society he came from and which is too prevalent in that subdivision don't accept mixing of the races. Strange, when half of them show definite black and Indio features. I think it was because he was married to her and she wasn't just some woman he had kids with. Weird. Judi

Clint thought about people he knew from the Penonomé area. That didn't seem to fit, but Judi mentioned the subdivision he was raised in, not the whole area. He knew there was still some bigotry against the Indigenos in some segments, particularly among the blacks. Judi mentioned mixed-race people and blacks specifically.

That didn't tell him much and told him a lot. He tended to respect people who could keep a good reputation while fighting societal stupidities.

Pretty obviously, he was going to have to learn what he could about this Generoso Flores L. It could have a hidden connection with the building materials if he had supplied anything for the finishing Martin did on the house.

He called Martin and asked if he used materials from Flores. He didn't know. The man who did the work, Edouard Hernandez, ordered things and he paid for them. He would look at the invoices and call back in the morning. The records for the house were at the office.

Not much else to do, so Clint walked into Bocas Town to chat with people and have a good dinner at the Nine Degrees.

In the morning Martin called just before eight thirty and said he did get some minor things from Flores, but only the normal kinds of things, and there wasn't any time he had spoken with Flores. The part about him not listening didn't make sense. He might have met Rudolfo Gomez. He slightly remembered someone who might have been him when his contractor was ordering something or other. He didn't remember speaking with him more than the normal greetings and "Mucho gusto."

"What kinds of things are on the invoice?" Clint asked.

"Let me see. Nails, Glue, electrical cable, iron pipe, pegboard, roof drain connectors, sink drains, toilet seals ... that's about it on this one.

"Next one is PVC, three quarter inch, PVC fittings, PVC glue, electrical cable, plumbing lead. That is a little bit strange. We carry PVC materials in my outlets.

"Next is roof flashing and electrical cable – we carry roof flashing, too. It seems Ed was making some deals on the side to purchase things that he could ... I have to check on what we delivered for him here."

"I spotted something a little strange, too," Clint replied. "It's all for plumbing or roof drains or such, but there were no electrical fittings, only cable."

"We carry all the electr ... and cable. Something is wrong here, Mr. Faraday! Why would he buy all that ... expensive! Number *eight* cable? We didn't use anything like number eight! We don't carry it! It's for commercial three phase trunk carriers! Twelve is as large as you use in a house! I don't understand why I didn't ... I didn't really read the things. I just gave him the money for it."

"That still doesn't come anywhere close to enough for him to make threats of ... what happened to that cable?

"I have another question. Why plumbing lead? It's not used anymore."

"It doesn't make sense. Ten five pound ingots of plumbing lead? If it was used, it wouldn't be more than a few ounces!"

Clint thought for a minute, then said, "I think I'll go to Panamá City. I want to know a thing or two about this Generoso Flores Lorenz. I just wish I could come up with a reason for all that heavy cable and ... heavy! Ten lead ingots!"

"I don't ...?"

"I once had a case where uranium was being smuggled out of the country, and later, one where plutonium was being smuggled in. I want to know what happened to that *heavy* cable and that *heavy* lead!"

There was a pause, then Martin said he had a Geiger counter from back when he and some friends were looking for radium when he was in university. He was going to check all around his place. He had small children there. If they were exposed to any such thing he was going to stop being Mr. Nice Guy to a couple of people. He was going to blow their goddamned fucking heads off for them!

He rang off, promising to call back as soon as he'd scanned the place. Clint started packing a few things and called for a flight to Panamá City. He could be on the one o'clock plane.

Martin called back at twelve thirty seven. There was no excess radiation anyplace on his property.

"I doubt the stuff ever got delivered to your place. Your Eddy-boy has, or had it."

"What should I do?"

"Nothing, for now. I'll check this out and call you as soon as I know anything. I suggest you collect your family together and either fortify yourselves into the house or go somewhere they can't find you.

"There may be no danger. Maybe Flores knows by now that he should be after Ed, not you. You can't take that chance."

"Mr. Faraday, I have just remembered something that may be important. It was from when I was introduced to Gomez. Ed said he was acting as my agent in all matters. Gomez nodded and said he was pleased to meet me, but knew everything in future was to be handled solely by Sr. Hernandez. I remember thinking that was a strange thing to say."

"Under the circumstances, it was to tell you that he understood that Ed was to handle things as a way to never have your name mentioned in the future, but also that he understood that you were the boss he was actually dealing with.

"I have to meet this Ed character. When I get back."

They made open plans for a few minutes and Clint rung off to get to his flight.

Clint left Albrook and headed toward the main city. He checked into the Hotel California, then had a good lunch at the chicken restaurant two blocks toward downtown, then took a taxi to the causeway. He would be looking for the Edificio GFL, according to the phone book.

It was a semi-highrise smoky glass and concrete building that had seen better days, but still wasn't in a state he could call run down.

He went into the lobby to read the directory board. GFL Ind. etc. was, of course, on the top two floors. It was much what he half expected it to be. Sort of in the successful but not ostentatiously so presentation. It wouldn't be watched too closely, because it was in the exact range that kind and size of a company should be if it was a straight-dealing type.

Clint looked around the place, and decided he had been wrong about any nuclear fuel idea. There weren't any occupants who would fit as a tie-in. Not in that area – which didn't mean whole lot, come to think of it. This wasn't the only office Flores had.

Was it?

He read the list of companies on the board. A stockbroker/trader, a freight airline company, two big food distributors, one meats and one vegetables, several civil lawyers, two empeños (loan companies), one a pawn shop type of affair. A designed clothing wholesaler and fine cloth and leathergoods dealer.

That pawn shop didn't quite fit until he saw it was one of four companies on the first floor. It would have an entrance from the sidewalk.

A restaurant and home electronics store were the other ground floor occupants.

A wholesale auto parts supplier and a florist supply company shared the second floor with a beauty parlor supply distributorship and a wine distributor.

The stockbroker and the pawn shop would just barely fit what he was looking for, which was some point from which he could begin his investigation.

He walked around the lobby for a few minutes, reading the ads on the wall for the occupants. He noted that the pawn shop was the standard type of thing, where the people running it could give small loans on cameras and TV's and so forth. The empeños dealt in gold and jewelry and the better collectibles. He remembered one who had the collectible sales bit who were using it to get uncut stolen emeralds out of Colombia. Copper and lead weren't collectibles.

But they were heavy. Gold was heavy.

There is a lot of gold in Panamá, but mostly in small veins. There were a few places where larger quantities were mined, and there were places on the comarcas that could be any size. There were a small number of the Indios who brought small quantities out, now and then. They only brought it when they were in special need of something that money was the only way to get. There were stories, but they were the same as anywhere you went in Central and South America. There was old pirate treasure, he had found some himself, but that wasn't something you could keep shut up for long. Manolo, his friend who was an secret agent for Interpol, heard about that kind of thing very quickly.

He called Manolo. There wasn't any movement of note lately.

Okay. He could work on the possibility there was a gold mine on a comarca that couldn't be worked legally ... but this wasn't making any sense. Flores was moving something heavy. It could be gold. It could be something else. There was silver.

An empeños company office was on the sixth

floor. That was moderately suspicious. Loan companies wouldn't be in places they wouldn't be noticed. There was a small ad in the lobby, nothing else.

He should be in Almirante or Changuinola, and he should be investigating Hernandez. The only reason Martin was at risk was because Hernandez had deliberately made Flores and Gomez think he was working strictly under orders from Martin.

That meant the product, whatever it was, was partly missing. Hernandez had it hidden somewhere and was planning on making a killing, because there could be no complaint with the police. He probably thought he was outsmarting a bunch of thieves. He could learn very suddenly and violently that these kinds of people didn't depend on the police for anything. He thought they would only concentrate on Martin. He never considered that he had established a chain with himself as a critical link, and that the chain could be broken at any link. Clint felt he was a link for him to look into. If the operation was big enough Hernandez could end up being the link where information stopped. All they had to do was eliminate that one link – and they would have no qualms about doing exactly that.

He had partly wasted his time coming to the city, but partly not. He felt he now did have a direction, and that it might not be exact, but was on the order of what was going on.

He called some people he knew from former visits and took them to dinner. He stayed at the hotel that night, got his things in the morning, and caught the early flight to Changuinola.

Clint called Martin and said he might have found a link, but couldn't be sure. He needed to talk with Hernandez. He got the celular number and called. Hernandez's wife said that he wasn't taking on anymore work right now. Clint said he needed some information about a job he'd already done. He didn't want to hire a job.

There was a pause and some loud angry voices at a distance he couldn't make out. The phone was turned off.

So. Maybe Hernandez had figured he was in a very tight spot.

His phone buzzed. Caller ID said it was the Hernandez number calling. He answered "Ola?"

"Sir, I am Edouard's wife. I am sorry, but he is drunk and can't answer the phone right now."

"Drunk? At nine thirty in the morning?"

"He has been drunk all night. I do not know why. I am afraid. He is never violent, but he has threatened to hit me."

"I can come and try to talk to him."

"No. I will go to my mother's house until he is sober. This will pass. I think he was cheated in the business. It will work out.”

“If you need help, call this number. I will do what I can.”

“Thank you.” She rung off.

Clint called Moises Silva and asked if he knew where Edouard Hernandez lived. He said it was because Hernandez was drunk and about to get violent with his wife.

“Out by the two rivers. Just past the first fork. There’s a sign about his business.

“What’s happening with him? He was here at this job four or five times in the past two months. He brought supplies for them or something, but this isn’t his job.”

“What kind of supplies?”

“I don’t know. He was taking boxes out of his van.”

“Thanks, Moises. This is getting confusing.”

“It is? What?”

“That’s what’s confusing. I don’t *know*!”

“That’s a big help!”

“I’m giving the phone the bird.”

“Me too!” They both laughed.

So. What was in those boxes? Was the problem that it wasn’t what was supposed to be?

Clint had to find what Edouard did with what was in the boxes. Moises was still at the job, so he could go there. Maybe Moises could get him into where they had the boxes, and he could see for himself. He drove out across the river and to the entrance road to the place. There was a guard, so he had him contact Moises, who said he was an expert consultant about a special problem. He was passed through.

Moises and his crew of four workers were the only ones there. That was a stroke of luck! He was shown where the boxes were unloaded into a steel container. There was a large padlock on each door, but Clint could pick that type easily – and did.

The container was neatly filled with all kinds of construction material. There was a narrow path down the center, and the stuff was stacked to the top to either side. Electrical was just past the center to the left. There were various boxes of cable, connectors, insulated tiedowns, and such. Clint suspected he was looking for number eight cable, and found twelve cartons. The legend said it was number eight copper, sixty six pounds per box. All the boxes had been opened, which said a lot. That kind of thing wasn't opened on a job until it was to be used.

He checked the cable. It was standard copper cable.

He then went on to the plumbing section. There

were ten lead ingots, five pounds apiece. The ends were cut into deeply on all of them. They were lead.

Fifty pounds of lead, 792 pounds of cable. Half a ton of whatever it was.

Moises was standing just outside. Clint asked if he had any surveying equipment, he said he had some. Nuclear? Yes. Did he have a leakage detector? Yes. He brought it.

Radiation levels were normal. Clint shook his head and Moises asked what was missing.

"I suspect it's half a ton of gold."

"Half a *ton*?!"

"Uh-huh. I think maybe it's going to be damned hard to keep Edouard alive for twenty four more hours."

"I see. We all know he's likely to steal things. He called it his early retirement fund. He stole the wrong thing this time."

"It would appear. I may be wrong, but I'm not. As for retirement, he may be permanently retired early."

He relocked the container and headed for the two river fork. Edouard was much too drunk to be coherent, and was as much as passed out. Clint asked his wife where he kept the stuff he stole. She got a tight look and asked what it was this time.

"Gold. He stole from the cartels or mob. Can you get him out of here and to a place he can't be found? Don't even tell me where."

She nodded and made a call on her celular. Her brother would come with the van truck and they would take him somewhere.

"There's a metal boat shed over the water in Almirante where he keeps things that are to go to the islands. That's all I know. I don't know where it is. I don't ever go to Almirante."

Clint thanked her and headed for Almirante.

Clint asked a lot of people where Edouard's boat shed was. They didn't know. It wasn't on the main canal to the water taxis and such.

He figured two places it could be on the water, so went back through Potter Town, but it wasn't on that short stretch, so went to the bridge on the way back toward the water taxis. He looked from the bridge to see several sheds, but only one was metal. That had to be it.

He noted the house beside it and went to ask the woman at the house if that was where Edouard kept his stuff for the islands. She said it was. Why?

"He's drunk and passed out. You can call his wife and she'll tell you that. I have to check some things to be sure they're ready."

"Then you have the key to get in. Go for it! I'm not responsible for that shed. I only rent him the space for it."

"Just wanted to let you know I'm not someone trying to rob him or something."

"I don't care if you are. You can't get in without the key or bolt cutters, and you don't have any bolt cutters. I'm not responsible."

He grinned at her and went along the little path beside the house to the shed, where he used his picks to get in quickly.

The place was crammed with the more expensive types of construction material. There were four of the gold-plated bathroom fixtures that sold for more than two hundred dollars each sitting on top of the boxes of number eight cable. The lead was sitting on them. It was scraped to where the gold showed.

Clint eased open a box of the electrical cable that had been opened before. The end of the wire was showing, and was bright gold colored.

Okay. He was right about that, but why? All he could think of was that the gold was from a place they weren't allowed to mine it or didn't own. It was an interesting way to move it, but risky. What happened might happen. He took one of the lead/gold bars and used a bolt cutter hanging on a peg to cut about a foot of the gold wire, then carefully resealed the box and left, hanging the big padlock the way it was when he opened it.

First order of importance was getting word to whoever that Martin had nothing to do with the theft, then to see what he could do about Edouard and keeping him alive. He could then concentrate on finding the source and exactly what was going on. He suspected some of his Indio friends were being robbed of that gold.

He got in his car and drove out to Martin's to explain what was going on. He didn't tell him he found anything except the "likely" thing that had happened. He didn't want him to know too much. It could be dangerous to him and his family.

Emilia brought them coffee, and sat to chat. Clint asked her if she was born on the comarca. She said she was.

"It was in a place where there is nothing the gringos would care about at all. It is beautiful tranquil mountains and forests and rivers. I was born in a small village near to Rio Guarenara. The closest town is Quebrada Tula, but that is a long way. "

"I've been to Quebrada Tula. I know the Luis Santinos family there, and a few others," Clint replied in Ngobe. "It is a beautiful place."

"Yes," she replied. "You speak Ngobe very well.

"We moved to Soloy when I was eleven. I lived there until I met Sam. He had been to Tula, and some people there told him about my family. He was coming to Soloy, and called my father. We met and he, as you gringos say, swept me off my feet. It was love from the start.

"He stayed in Soloy for only two days, but my

heart was broken when he must leave. He could not stay away, and came back in only three more days and asked me to marry him. I was over-joyed. We went to Quebrada Tula to become married in the Ngobe tradition, then to David for the ceremony in the church there.

"Sam does not follow the religion, but it is tradition in his family to become married by the church.

"We lived for several years in Penonomé and came here, where Sam has the business. I like this place very much, and there are many of my people close. I am teaching my children how to respect my culture, and they are teaching me to respect the Latin culture.

"It is very strange. Everything here is so very good, but there are differences in the culture, even among my own people here that I cannot become accustomed to. I sometimes find myself missing the life when I was a child of eight or nine. I had my duties in the family that the Latin people do not have. Their children seem to be so ... without purpose is, I think, a way to express it. I had a definite purpose, a duty to my family, that they lack. I think it makes them unhappy and feeling not ... safe in life."

"True. They are insecure. I hope your children are not?"

"My children have a purpose to the family and the duties that are expected of those who have that purpose. We laugh and play as we work, and we enjoy the fact that we can live and feel. We are free within our own spirits."

"In short, your children are Ngobe, know it, and are proud that they have a place in that culture. The Latins don't have a place and don't know if they ever will. That's scary for a child. They don't even know why they feel that way."

"They will always seek and seldom find," she agreed. "They never know who they are."

"That's, sadly, the basic truth," Sam said. "I didn't understand at first why the kids didn't demand an allowance. They didn't know why anyone would give anything to someone who was only living their life as it was meant.

"I was raised to think I was a very special person who would someday be rich and famous. There was no basis, foundation, to support that idea. When I was fifteen or sixteen, I often felt useless and alone, even when I was with fifty friends. I never knew why.

"Now I do. I am greatly confused by what I once wanted – and got! – and what is now most important to me.

"My family is the most important thing in my life, not being rich and famous. I no longer *want* to be rich and famous! I have much more than most. I don't want even more. That empty feeling is gone. It does not have to be filled with useless *things*.

"I so very deeply regret the things I have done before in search of money and power. I have this because I wanted it. Now it is here and I would much rather be ... somewhere else."

"You know what this is really about, don't you? You're in a trap you can't find a way out of."

"Mr. Faraday, I wish to speak with you about some things I am not proud of. Things I am ashamed of. I do not wish to involve my family in this mess. I called you because I was told you are accepted by my wife's people as one of them, and that you are known to help people in trouble."

Clint nodded. "Shall we go for a drive?"

"I understand," Emilia said quietly. "I think I have learned some things, and that you may help us. Sam has told me a little."

They stood. Sam and Clint went to his car and drove to sit on a gravel fill by the road where the magnificent view of the islands was before them. Sam said he didn't know where to start.

"The gold is from the comarca near Quebrada Tula." It was a statement by Clint.

"Okay. The entire story, from the start," Sam promised. "I won't leave anything out to protect myself. I desperately need help in a way that will not leave a bigger burden on my soul.

"I could easily hire people to kill them. I could not live with that, though I think they wouldn't hesitate a minute if they didn't know they must have me."

<u>*A Life Story*</u>

"It started when I was in my early teens and had been raised to think money and power were the answer to all questions in life. My life had little of worth in it, in any real sense. We were middle class, and had some things. My father was always in debt, usually because he bought some useless bit of furniture or, I once remember when I was about nine or ten, a car that kept him in debt for four years. It was to impress the neighbors. Most of them did the same things. I remember that I thought it was so phony, trying to impress people who were trying to impress you, and all doing the same thing, so no one was impressed.

"He joined a union that promised him a better salary and better conditions. He thought it was really great, because he got about ten dollars a week more. He soon became worried because he was paying part of the increase in dues to the union. Prices soon went up enough to eat up his salary increase without that. The actual result was that he lost.

"He felt that gave him the right to screw his employers, through some truly illogical thought process. Now he was getting ahead of his bills because he became a thief. One of the few times he ever hit me was when I said being a common thief was hardly a way to impress the neighbors.

"He got caught and spent three months in jail. He couldn't find a job when he got out, and he owed money to almost everyone he knew.

"He jumped off a bridge in the mountains onto the rocks. The river was almost dry.

"I became bitter, then. My father chased after something silly his whole life and never found peace, and certainly not the respect he thought he could buy. He looked at his life, at the end. He had nothing, he had become a thief, he owed everyone, no one trusted him. He killed himself.

"I vowed that I was going to get those things my father wanted. I was going to find a way to get super rich and get my revenge on the world. I was going to be rich and famous and powerful.

"Politics! Everyone could see that if you got even the most minor office you became rich very quickly. All you needed was a little education and a line to tell the people.

"I got a job in a political party office when I was eighteen. I met the candidates, and even knew about a few little transgressions, mainly about the fact some of them had two or three families in other nearby towns that didn't know anything about each other. I began to peddle some influence. I bought a new car. I wore fancy clothes and expensive shoes and had some gold jewelry. I had women chasing me because they thought I was rich.

"I saw that I was in the trap my father had been in. I was doing a lot of it on credit I as much as blackmailed people into granting me. It couldn't sustain. Someone would eventually get caught and they'd surely take me down with them if they couldn't make me the goat. I was being used. They were laughing at me.

"I met an Indio who has a little bit of gold he wanted to sell to pay for the hospital treatment for his wife. He brought the gold to Penonomé because he heard that there was someone there, someone in local politics, who would buy the gold and not tell the government. A Mr. Garcia.

"I had some things on Garcia. I made a deal with him to find where the gold came from, and we'd both get richer than the famous Midas!

"I bought the gold from the Indio and acted concerned about his sick wife. I went to the hospital to ingratiate myself to them. I had paid enough for the hospital from gold that was worth three times that. He would be better off giving the government half.

"His wife was healed and ready to go home, but

they had no money for the bus fare. I said she shouldn't be riding on a bus. She had been too sick recently. Out of the goodness in my heart I would pay for a taxi to take them right to their front door!

"They said a taxi couldn't get there, but it could get closer than the bus. That was good enough. I could learn exactly where they found the gold.

"I was deeply affected by my close contact with those two Indios. Jon, who I named my son after, was a natural, friendly, good person who didn't understand the ways of money and power. He was confused by it, and couldn't understand why there was a charge for medical help for people who needed it. He couldn't understand why food cost so much. He couldn't understand why he and his wife weren't invited to someone's house when he was in need. After all, wasn't he also a person?

"I was affected. I could see this was a good man, and I respected him greatly, even though he had no money or possessions, and certainly no power. He was just an honest normal man.

"I later figured what it was. He retained dignity throughout his problems. He was in a strange and scary society, and retained his sense of personal worth – which was the same as anyone else's worth. No more, certainly no less.

"In other words, he had self-respect. My father never had that, and I never had that. It occurred to me that I didn't respect any of these money and power people. I merely envied them, to an extent. I had no self-respect, therefore I could not expect anyone else to respect me. I thought of the people I *showed* respect for. I didn't respect them. Some, I feared. Others I sneered at behind their backs.

"I determined I was never going to be one of them. I would find a way to escape that meaningless circular trap.

"I had the one major problem; I knew no other way than to get a lot of money. That was there before me, but I swore to the god I don't believe in that I would never again harm another person, most certainly not Jon. I seemed to understand that meant Jon and his people.

"One thing happened that I will never forget. There was another Ngobe there who had lived in Penonomé for a year or less, and who made his living by collecting aluminum cans and cutting people's grass. He had nothing, but was content. He was someone you greeted on the streets, and didn't consider his station.

"I was shocked at myself! I actually thought that! His *station*!

"Anyway, he had nothing, and Jon had nothing and no way to make a few dollars. Obilio talked with him about the situation with his wife. He had no food, and was sleeping on a cardboard box in a shed near the hospital.

"Obilio took him along to collect aluminum cans and cut a woman's lawn. Altogether they made less than ten dollars. Obilio gave it *all* to Jon. I asked him why he didn't keep part of it, and he couldn't understand the question. Jon was his people.

"I never really felt I was even a part of my own family. This man was a part of all his people! He had a place and reason, I had neither.

"I changed profoundly. My problem became that I still only knew to accumulate money, and I would, supposedly, then have all the rest. It was suddenly obvious to me that I was a fool. I would never have all the rest. It was from inside of me, and there was nothing inside me. I thought much about this.

"Jon returned to his home with his wife. I was invited to come to live with them when I found the city didn't have anything to offer except greed and impersonality and pollution and noise.

"I met with Garcia about two weeks later and made arrangement to go to a little village called Quebrada Tula. I would then go to other parts of the comarca. He would finance the trip, though the whole thing didn't cost a hundred dollars for a three week circuit of the comarca.

"I went. I was to use subtlety and trickery to find where the gold was.

"I stayed in Tula, most of the time, that first trip, and saw trinkets of pure gold in many places. I asked about it, and was told it was taken from the river. There were spots where there was enough to make a small ring or a locket or something. One could sometimes find enough to pay for a trip into a city, but most found that once was enough of that. It did not suit the Indigenos.

"I made one trip on the river in a cayuca with two brothers who had become my friends.

"For the first time in my life I could say people I met and knew for only a day could be friends. Few of the people I had known my entire life could be called friends in the sense it means with the Indigenos.

"I found a place where a stream that was strong in the more wet seasons met the river. There was a fair amount of gold there. I managed to collect more than four ounces in less than an hour.

"I went back to Penonomé with that four ounces of gold and got cash for it from a person who deals in gold. It was more than two thousand dollars! For one hour!

"I knew a man who owned a small furniture store and feriteria who died while I was gone. His wife wanted to sell the business. I gave her the two thousand and promised to pay two more when I had it. I did that quite soon. I was now in business, and could begin my plan to make a lot of money.

"Garcia insisted that we could shortcut the time. I could go back and arrange to get a lot of that gold. He would send a man with me who was born on the comarca, so could communicate with the Indios. He would gather gold quietly and store it until we had a great quantity. We would then find a way to move it away from Penonomé. He knew a person in Limón, Costa Rica, who was originally from Colombia who could handle any amount of gold. It would be one time, so we must collect as much as we could.

"The man who traveled with me to Quebrada Tula was Fredrico Sandanias. He stayed there until one month ago.

"We gathered almost fifty pounds of gold then, and moved it as planned. I was wealthy, Garcia was wealthy, Sandanias was wealthy.

"I invested the money and built a large and comfortable business so that – but I am getting ahead of myself, now.

"I made two more trips to Tula, and made stops on the way back. Each time I had become more enamored with the Indigenos and their free lifestyle. They are also a very handsome people, and the women with their long shiny black hair and skin of purest rare satin were my dream mate.

"On the next to last trip I was in Soloy when I mentioned Tula. A friend said he knew a family living right there who were from the area. He introduced me to Emilia and her parents and two brothers. I was attracted to Emilia a bit more than my general attraction to the people.

"She described where she was raised. It was land very close to where Fredrico had discovered the source of the gold in the steam. It was a large and open cavern in the side of a rocky mountain where almost no one ever went. They don't care about gold, and there is nothing in that area. It is not easy to get there.

"I suddenly had a plan! The family had a house very close to the place that wasn't being used. I was welcome to stay there as long as I wanted. That included my closer friends, in the way the Indigenos express such things. I could then move Fredrico into the house and he could spend a lot more time gathering the gold!

"You see, we had decided to let things go along for awhile and to collect more of the gold, then we could make one more deal. We felt we could very probably get two to three hundred pounds of gold, a true fortune!

"I immediately went back to Tula and moved Fredrico into the house. I then returned to Soloy, where I couldn't think of anything except Emilia. I felt it would be good business to date her. It would insure we could stay at that house without future problems.

"I did date her. I liked her more than anyone I had ever before known.

"I had to go to Panamá City to register some legal papers having to do with the businesses I owned. I was soon going to open a new store in Changuinola. I had always liked Bocas del Toro. I wanted to see if there was a residence close where I could live.

"I couldn't stay away. I thought I was worried that someone else would take Emila as a novia, and things could get bad.

"That wasn't why, but I didn't know that until later. I only knew I was attracted to Emilia more than anyone before, and that it would be good business to somehow solidify the relationship. I was back into the idea of money being respect and power again, if not nearly so strongly. After all, it was the way I was raised.

"I hoped Emilia would consider a long-term relationship that could lead to marriage. I made the proposal, and she accepted. I had never known such pure joy and elation in my life! It was the point where I knew I couldn't live the kind of life I was trapped into.

"I told her only a couple of years ago that I had schemed to marry her for the wrong reasons, but that I had immediately fallen totally in love with her, and still am.

"That was about fourteen years ago. I had little contact with Garcia, and maybe once a year with Fredrico. I felt they would take the gold, maybe they already had, and I'd be free of them. The people on the comarca wouldn't care about the gold, so long as it didn't result in a bunch of greedy strangers coming to try to take their land like they had done in several places before when something was found.

"I suddenly got a call from Garcia. He is sick and about to die, but his son has taken over his end of the deal. His son is a bigshot politician in Panamá City, some kind of representative sent from Penonomé.. I have discovered he is keeping the family tradition of being corrupt snakes.

"Garcia said Fredrico had all the gold he wanted to spend time on. He wanted to travel the world and know other things and other places. He had a thousand pounds ready to bring in. They had cast the gold, first into five pound ingots they had covered with lead. It could be transported as plumbers' lead. The rest was cast as electrical cable. Garcia owned a place that extruded – I think that is what they call it – wiring copper. It would be a simple thing to coat it as standard cable and match the weight to the boxes. No one would ever know. They could deliver real cable and exchange it later for the gold. The person who handled it was building a casino and brothel near Changuinola. That was a crossing they could use to get the gold to Costa Rica. One thousand pounds was twelve thousand ounces of twenty four karat gold. Gold was then selling for around one thousand five hundred dollars an ounce. We got eighty percent. That was eighteen million dollars to be split three ways. They had made an arrangement with my contractor, who was building my house here. He was to receive ten thousand dollars cash for simply delivering the gold to the job near Changuinola and taking the real cable and lead away.

"Edouard had made a deal that sounded like he was taking orders strictly from me. I did not know about it until just a few days ago when the gold was delivered to Edouard and never to the job.

"I was contacted by Garcia, who said I had agreed in front of his agent that Edouard was taking his orders from me. I said that is not what I understood. He said it was to me to clear it up and to deliver that gold. He gave me three days. On the morning of the third day I got the wreath.

"Mr. Faraday, I want my family protected. I believe it will not be possible to protect me, but they are innocent. I have no fear of dying, if my family are safe. They are the entire reason for my life. It is my all."

"It's Clint, and I think we can do something about this mess. I want Garcia's and Fredrico's numbers."

"I don't have them."

"Did Garcia call your cel number?"

"Yes! It will be in the received calls list!" He took out his personal celular and went through the numbers. "It was the call after Rodelaq and just before the Smith call. They were close, so it will be this one."

"Call him! Place it through privado. He won't know who's calling that way, and I can pull a bluff."

Martin set the "hide caller ID" button and handed Clint the phone. It rang four times, then the "leave a message" tone. Clint said he would call at exactly eleven o'clock. It was important and was about the gold.

"That's just six minutes from now. We can discuss a couple of things about making sure your family's safe," Clint said. "You can still use that house on the comarca?"

"Yes, but won't they know we're there?"

"Not if I ask the people to not tell anyone that."

"They respect you greatly. Emilia says you were made a Ngobe by order of the council."

"Yes. It was one of the proudest moments of my life."

He nodded. "I think that, now that I understand what the culture is and what the people are, it would be the crowning event of my life."

"I think Emilia could arrange that. It would mean your children are pure Ngobe."

They chatted for a few minutes. Clint took the celular exactly at eleven and made his call. It was answered on the second ring.

"Sr. Garcia? I represent a group. I must explain a few things to you. Call them the facts of life.

"You are not dealing with Samuel Martin anymore. He wishes to be free of you. He thought he already was.

"I became involved in this when a man got drunk yesterday and ran his mouth in front of someone who just happened to be there because of his earlier dealings with another such group who are building a casino and whorehouse on the river in Changuinola.

"I investigate things for various people. It was easy enough to trace back and find that Martin had actually been duped into this part of the deal. We know about the earlier movement. If we know, you can deduce who we are.

"We are able to pay eighteen million in cash for this deal with cash on hand. That should tell you how impressed we are with your little business.

"We can see the gold is delivered to you to where you can produce what was promised. It takes a promise from you that will be honored so long as there is a you. Should the promises not be honored, your life will be a short one.

"I am aware the original deal was with your father (Martin shook his head). You can see we know a great deal more about you and this than you would ever guess.

"We do not bluff. Shall the gold be delivered with your promise to forget there was ever a deal with anyone and with the guarantee that people no longer involved will not become involved again with anything to do with you – ever?"

"You don't scare me! Who are you? What is this? I don't know what you're talking about!"

"Yet you answered the call," Clint snarled. "Look around you. Do you see the two men who are ignoring your existence just ahead and to your right? They are talking together?"

"Er?"

Clint had heard the background noises, and

knew Garcia was outside somewhere. There were enough indistinct voices to make it a good bet there were two men talking somewhere to his right.

"Think about if I were to say something into this celular in my other hand that resulted in a distraction that called attention to them while you had a fatal accident just when everyone turned away?"

There was a short pause. "I see. You represent ... that Colombian bunch?"

"I represent many people at many times. It is what I do. I'm not cheap, and I'm definite."

"Have you considered that Martin will know about all of it?"

"He does now. He's simply tried hard to stay away from the type of business. He doesn't want or need anymore millions. He makes it legitimately. You can keep his part of the deal, and it will never again arise in conversation, public or private. It is something that never happened."

"I wish I could believe that."

"I can guarantee it. I am not known for being mistaken in such matters. Not ever. Making me wrong would make the one who guaranteed it to me a footnote in past history."

"I see. It can be that, or I am the footnote."

"You said it. I didn't."

"Not in so many words. The message has been delivered. You have my word."

"That is all I ask."

"I'll be damned!"

"Beg pardon?"

"I was convinced this was some ... I give the promise, and the two walk away ten seconds later! It was real!"

"I never go back on my word. I hope it's not necessary to ever contact you again. You must make clear to Freddy-boy that this applies to him, as well."

"Understood. I can handle him. He was never convinced that Martin was involved in it."

"Have a nice life, Sr. Garcia."

"You, too. I'll retire to my little place near San Andreas. I can resign my job for personal and health reasons."

"Which is the truth, in a roundabout way."

"Yes, it is, isn't it?" He rang off.

"You're truly amazing! You actually had some people there?! How did you know?!"

"No. I heard background noises, which tells a detective that he was outside or in a crowded area. As the call was one that *must* not be overheard, it was a good bet it was outside. When you're outside in a park or on the streets, it's a very safe bet that somewhere ahead and to your right there are two men talking to one another. That they left at that particular moment was a stroke of purest luck."

"I can well see why you're so successful as a detective. You play the odds in a way that they can almost always be counted on to fall your way. If there weren't those two men there, what would you say?"

"That my perspective was from a Blackberry camera, and it could as well be that they were to his left or even a little bit behind him. With the number of voices I could hear in the background, there were probably two men talking no matter which direction he looked."

"Well, do you think I should go to Quebrada Tula with my family?"

"Yes. Make it a vacation. You might decide it's too good a place to come back from."

"I've thought that I would like to live in such a place part of the year and here part of the year. That is now a viable option, I think."

"I would say it is. Let's go back and tell your wife she is going home for a visit."

"My children will be there for the lunch time. I would like for them to meet you."

"I want to meet them." He started the car.

Clint went to Moises' job and asked that he come along. He would supply two men to load some stuff to take to the job he was working on.

"And I am not to remember going anywhere and getting anything?"

"To what, whither thou goest, doest thou refer henceforth?"

That got him a grin and the finger.

He drove them to Almirante, where Clint went to several Indios at the end dock of the water taxi channel. He said he had a job for them and their cayuca. Stack the plaintains at one end and come with him to the second river. He and Moises rode with them to the shed, where Clint opened the lock and had them load on all the cable and lead. They covered the boxes with the plaintains and went back to load the boxes into his car. He drove to the job, where he and Moises took the cable into the container and took out the real items. He thought about it and said, "What the hell!" and put the real cable into the container at the end. Why should Edouard get it when he stole so much stuff, anyway?

At the end, Clint saw a black plastic package that could too easily be cocaine. He opened the corner and saw packages of hundred dollar bills. He thought a minute, then slid out a packet of fifty. They were new and in series. That didn't seem quite right for a laundering operation, but could be. He slipped the packet into his pocket. Moises was outside, so didn't see him.

He soon left Moises there with his crew and headed back into Changuinola. The people building the casino were in Costa Rica, but would be back later in the afternoon. Clint booked into a hotel and cleaned up, called his wife to find she and Judi were back on Isla Colón, and that everything was going very well. His nutty musician/botanist/author close friend, Dave, had come back from Almirante on the same boat and was there, having coffee. Clint talked with him and asked if he'd ever been to Quebrada Tula. He didn't know where it was, and Clint said on the comarca in the middle of nowhere, which meant it would be a paradise. He explained about the case.

"Emilia? Married to that Sam guy who owns a lot of stores or something? I know them. She's turned Sam into an Indio. Their kids are a contrast with the Latina culture if there ever was one. I also think, besides the fact they're so goodlooking, that everyone envies them for their great life. They're happy kids, with a strong ingrained sense of responsibility."

"In other words, Ngobe."

"Something like that. They manage to fit into both societies. That's because Mom figured the best way to fit into both and taught them and Poppa how to live."

"Self-respect. I talked it over with Sam."

"Yeah. He got where he was always aiming for and found he didn't much like it. He's got a lot of money that doesn't mean anything anymore. He's happy because he learned the difference in price and value, and because he's learned that respect is earned, never given.

"Philosophy time's over. We've both heard it a thousand times before. Yes. I'd like to go to Quebrada Tula. It should be a fascinating place for my new studies." He was a botanist with a specialty in orchids, which were almost everywhere you looked in Panamá. Dave discovered dozens of species that weren't listed as being found in Panamá and a couple more that were, apparently, new classifications.

"I take it you were about to ask me that."

"I probably would have. I'm undecided, but the way Emilia and her kids turned out, I think it might be a good place for Tyna and me to be when the baby's born."

"You'd go nuts in six months. You're dreaming again.

"So! Why are you going to stay in Changuinola tonight when it's so close to home?"

"I want to make a few things clear to some people."

"That Colombian crowd is learning it's a lot smarter to work without involving people who don't go into it with their eyes wide open. It can backfire on them when they forget that."

"That, and I want to warn them about mixing their little deals."

"Mixing them? I don't see what they could be mixing. They're just buying gold at eighty percent market in a boringly typical money laundering scheme, so there has ... funny money?"

"I'd say so. Damned good, but it looks all too possible. I want to be sure."

"So? Let them screw each other. Who cares?"

"I don't want a few million in bogus hundreds floating around this end of Panamá. Too many innocent people get burned."

"I see. Maybe it would be a good way to send a message to them that it can be traced and could lose the geetus and the gold, both."

"I hadn't even considered that. I don't care

about the laundering around that bunch of half-assed hoods and corrupt crooks. The legitimate money isn't backed up with anything anymore, but this ends up with some poor schnook who sells his car or land or whatever getting the shaft. Keep it in Panamá City and Colón and nobody cares. Bring it here, and I care. These are my people who are getting screwed."

"Don't get on another soap box. You can make them move it to somewhere else and bring in good currency here. It won't even inconvenience them much."

Clint talked with Tyna again, then rang off. He had to be at the Grande Central Hotel at eight for his dinner. The people he wanted to see would be there. Jorge Residio and Herve Namas.

He cleaned up, put part of the bills in his wallet, and went to the dining room to order the lasagna he heard was good. Jorge and Herve came in at ten after and went to their usual table, next to where Clint was sitting. He nodded at them and waited until they all finished their meals, then went to ask if he could have a word. Herve waved to a chair. Clint ordered a drink for all of them.

"Clint Faraday. We were told we might meet you one day. We tend to draw attention because of the business we're building," Jorge said. "It's all above the table. It's legal here, and we have all the necessary permits – but you don't care about that.

"So? What's the problem?"

"I want to avoid a problem. I want to tell you the gold's in the container and that everything's been taken care of. The problem was because of a misunderstanding. Martin was never any part of this one. That was a suggestion made by Edouard to make it look like he was taking orders from Martin if he got caught.

"He's learned his lesson. If you do anything more it will only result in a lot of things coming out that nobody wants to come out, mostly you. Second, don't use the phony money on this one. Not here. Do that on the other end of the country. Leave things as they lay now with those stipulations, and we won't ever have to get in each other's way again, hopefully."

"I agree, totally, but there is no phony money involved. I swear it!"

Clint opened his wallet and dropped ten of the bills from the packet on the table. "So. Now I know exactly how far I can trust or believe you."

Herve looked confused and Jorge shocked. That seemed to be real.

"But ... these are phony? They look ... they're not phony!"

"I can't find that they are, but that's a lot of money to be in series like that. Explain that and I'll go away."

Herve carefully studied the bills. He took a magnifying lense from his pocket and spent several minutes studying the bills.

"They're good. I don't know why they're in series. Let me make a call?"

He went outside for about ten minutes while Clint and Jorge chatted. He came in to say, "They're good. The bank was ... oh. You're not up on the more recent innovations in the business.

"We get the money directly from the American bank branches in Bogota. The cash. There are electronic deposits to the bank by various business concerns within the country. We have branches in every small town or village that each deposit an amount such a business would collect in a time period. Some are as little as a thousand dollars per week, some are for a million every three days. Larger casinos and so forth. They are all licensed registered businesses. We do not deal with counterfeit money anymore. We leave that kind of thing to the smaller scale ... corporations. Our deposits are within the expectations of the individual business. We pay all taxes on those monies."

"The thing is that the businesses exist only on paper?"

"Not even there. They exist electronically. We even have an advertising concern on the net that garners some millions per month."

"That is paid to you from the casinos you own and so forth. You actually place a lot of ads."

"Exactly. Business methods are changing."

"That's okay, then. I only wanted to be sure the little man who busts his hump to raise a family doesn't get screwed because of some scheme run by a bunch of sleazy millionaire crooks."

Jorge laughed. "Flattery will get you nowhere!"

"The truth's not flattery."

"Welcome to today's world," Herve said, with a tight smile. "Sometimes I greatly regret that."

"It takes the excitement from much of it," Jorge agreed. "I find I have all this money and virtual castles in several countries and servants who bow and scrape because I leave a weeks' wages in one tip. It used to be exciting, because we were in actual danger, but now we learn that killing or maiming someone will come back on you, so we live boring lives. We can't trust any woman, and know damned well that no one respects us, they pretend to so they can con us out of some money.

"I think I'm sick to death of money! The whole thing's a teenager's silly dream! Women and cars and parties and fame! Wealth up the ying-yang! People begging for the chance to even get to know you!

"The women are only after the money. The respect's false. The wild parties are with a bunch of lonely people who bore each other talking about money and adventures that never happened except on TV. People clambering to know you so they can maybe get a couple of dollars off of you. It's total *bullshit!* You get to where you wish you were back in Lower Puddleville and sixteen again so you could maybe have a life! All it would take is for you to be able to know what life was really like, at that age.

"I guess it's just part of the way of the world anymore. God, but I'm bored! I have more fun here with the regular people who don't know who I am and don't give a flying shit than I do with these so-called high class society types who can only talk about their cars and boats and houses and bank accounts. I can buy this whole town for cash, and it doesn't mean *shit* to me anymore!

"I guess you can see I'm affected a lot."

"I'm not," Herve said. "I guess I know a little about how he feels. When you get down to it, you feel the same, with or without the money. The money makes it easier to tolerate life. It sort of gives you something to do. I only keep the money to see if I can wrack up the highest score in life. For itself, I agree. It's bullshit."

"I talk with your friend, Moises, at the job. He seems amused by us. I told him he could really make a lot of money if he'd do a couple of things. He said he has enough and he has something to do he can be proud of, and he has a family to carry on after he's gone. What more could any-one want from life?

"He laughs a lot, and I see even the ones who work with him hug him like a long-lost brother when they come to work in the morning.

"I don't ever remember hugging another man like that. It's so natural to them."

"They care about each other. You don't. That's something that comes from when you were two months old until you're grown, which is about twelve or thirteen years, among the Indios," Clint explained. "They have an inclusive culture. I've been thinking a lot about that lately. My wife's having a baby in about four months. I want to raise it right."

"You're considered an Indio?" Herve said. "I think Moises said that. I saw you talking with him over in Changuinola a couple of months ago, and how you were hugging everyone the same way they do.

"I was ... I've noticed that the Blacks' and

Latins' children are always arguing and running wild in public, and that you never see that in the Indios. Maybe raising children the Indio way is better. I don't know."

"It can't be artificial," Clint said. "My wife's also a Ngobe. I'm undecided if I should take them away from the Latin/Gringo culture until they're ten years old or something."

"I damned well would if I had the chance with my own kids – if I ever have any," Jorge said. "I wonder if I could have happy kids, like I never was."

They chatted about raising children for awhile. When Clint left, he didn't feel quite so negative about them as when he first came to the restaurant, expecting a confrontation.

It seemed the world actually was changing. It was May of 2012. Maybe the Mayan calendar was going to be more accurate than he had ever believed. Maybe there would be some enormous and radical changes to the world, not in cataclysms, but in how people lived.

Clint looked at Tyna, his wife, as she went about the house, doing the things housewives did the world over, and felt warm all over. She was a beautiful woman, and intelligent. They were here in Cusapín, visiting friends.

They had discussed raising the children in the Indio culture, not the Latina/Gringo mishmash. They hadn't completely decided, but were close to doing so.

Cusapín was paradise, and in the comarca. Clint was declared a Ngobe. Tyna was Ngobe. Their children would be Ngobe. This was a great place to raise children with a sense of value and self-respect.

Dave had just called from Quebrada Tula and said Clint would love the place. He had been to the gold mine, and said it had a few hundred tons of the stuff in a quartz seam. It would be very easy to mine the way Fredrico had been mining it, if anyone was interested.

Nobody was. It could stay there and the Indios could use it in emergencies.

Maybe Clint could have a sort of roving life

with his wife and children. Move around on the comarca most of the time, and take the children to town maybe twice a year when they were older.

Basilio came to talk a bit. He was one of the two chiefs who declared that Clint was Ngobe. It seemed Dave had left quite a collection of orchids with quite a number of the people and Cusapín was getting the reputation of being a botanist's dream. He said maybe they would call it Orquidias and attract a lot of tourists.

"You do and I'll never come near the place again! It would turn Cusapín into Bocas Town Two!"

Basilio laughed. There were a few tourists who came to Cusapín for the many miles of fantastic beaches and fishing and surfing. Basilio tolerated them, but didn't care to attract tourists. All they would bring to the place was greed and arrogance and crime.

They talked of mostly nothing and joked for awhile, then Clint walked along the wide white beach with Tyna as the sun set over the mountains to the west.

A long way toward the west. The sunset was spectacular.

He hugged her tightly to himself and felt the glow she always brought to him. He was happy here. She was happy here. Maybe they would raise their children here.

As the light faded, they walked slowly back to town and to the neat little cabin by the water. Clint felt he had no right to be so totally content with life as he was.

He wasn't about to give it up for one second, regardless!

C. D. Moulton's works are available on most major outlets as printed or e-books. CD writes the CD Grimes, PI mysteries, the Det. Lt. Nick Storie mysteries, the Clint Faraday mysteries, the Flight of the Maita science fiction series, books on orchid culture and many others of many types. Mystery, adventure, intrigue, science fiction, fantasy, para-normal, mild erotica, and factual.